Kathryn White

Gill Guile

PRESS THE PAGE
HEAR THE NOISE!

The Very Noisy Jungle

Intercourse, PA 17534, 800/762-7171, www.GoodBooks.com

All was calm in the jungle when Whiz
the parrot glided on to a branch.

"Caw, everything's so quiet," he moaned.
"This jungle needs some noise!"

Sq

uawk!

Flapping his wings and sticking out his tail, Whiz shrieked so high that the leaves shivered on the trees.

Pop the little monkey was hanging upside down when he heard Whiz shout.

"Oh, no! Whiz is in trouble!" he thought. "Crocodile must be snapping at him with his big, sharp teeth."

"I'm coming, Whiz!" called Pop, as he sprang across the treetops.

Pop rushed up to Whiz. “I thought Crocodile was chasing you!” he cried.

“There’s no crocodile,” said Whiz. “But did you hear my squawk? Bet you can’t shriek like me!”

Squawk!

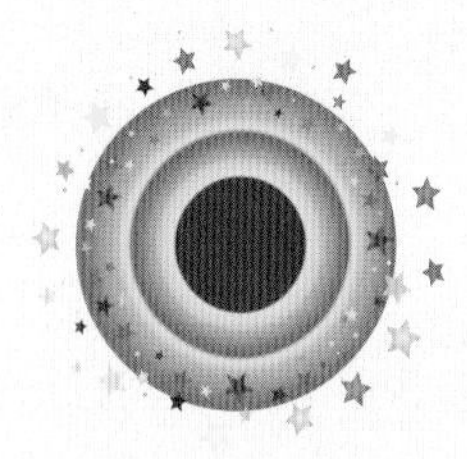

"Silly Whiz," said Pop. "My screech is much better." Pop crossed his eyes, took a deep breath and screeched so high that the trees trembled and shook.

Screech!

Peanut the little elephant was splashing in the river when he heard Whiz and Pop cry out.

"Oh, no! What if sly Snake has tied my friends in knots?" thought Peanut.

"Peanut's coming!" he shouted, and he thundered through the jungle as fast as his little legs could carry him.

Peanut came crashing up to his friends.
"I ran all the way here to save you
from Snake," he panted.

"Snake isn't here," chuckled Whiz. "But isn't my squawk fantastic?"

Squawk!

"My screech is louder," chattered Pop.

Screech!

"Well, listen to this!" said Peanut,

Trumpeting!

Flapping his ears and wiggling his tail, he blew so hard that the trees trembled and shook, and the ground rumbled.

"Wasn't that amazing?
My trumpeting is as loud as thunder!" snorted Peanut.

"That's nothing. My screech echoes for miles," boasted Pop.

"My squawk is so high I can wake the whole jungle," snapped Whiz.

Flapping and scrapping, no one could agree whose sound was best. So they raced off to ask Rory the tiger.

"What's all that noise?" asked Rory.

"We can't decide whose sound is best," said Whiz in a flap. "Listen!"

Squawk!

Screech!

Trumpeting!

"It's obvious!" said Rory. "The mightiest noise belongs to ME!"

Growl!

Rory growled so loudly that the trees trembled and shook, and the ground rumbled and rocked.

Squawk!

Screech! Trumpeting! Growl!

Feathers flew
and whiskers quivered as
everyone tried to make
the loudest noise.

All of a sudden, someone let out a cry
so piercing that the friends stopped arguing
in a flash!

"Oh, no! We've woken my baby sister,"
said Rory, "and now she's crying!
We'll be in SUCH trouble!"

Wa

aaaaaaahh!

Just then, the leaves wobbled and swayed . . .

. . . as Mommy Tiger leaped out.

"She's angry," Rory squealed. "Quick, everybody, HIDE!"

Then the animals trembled from their heads to their toes, as Mommy Tiger let out the loudest noise of all . . .